Mirror Magic

Acknowledgments
Executive Editor: Diane Sharpe
Supervising Editor: Stephanie Muller
Design Manager: Sharon Golden
Page Design: Ian Winton
Photography: The Robert Harding Picture Library: cover (left), page 29; Alex Ramsay: pages 9, 11, 17; Tony Stone Worldwide: cover (top and bottom right), pages 23, 27; Zefa: pages 15, 25.

ISBN 0-8114-3769-8

Copyright © 1995 Steck-Vaughn Company.

All rights reserved. No part of the material protected by this copyright may be reproduced or utilized in any form or by any means, electronic or mechanical, including photocopying, recording, or by any information storage and retrieval system, without permission in writing from the copyright owner. Requests for permission to make copies of any part of the work should be mailed to: Copyright Permissions, Steck-Vaughn Company, P.O. Box 26015, Austin, TX 78755.
Printed in the United States of America.
British edition Copyright © 1994 Evans Brothers.

1 2 3 4 5 6 7 8 9 00 PO 00 99 98 97 96 95 94

Mirror Magic

Alex Ramsay

Illustrated by
Stuart Trotter

Steck-Vaughn
COMPANY
ELEMENTARY · SECONDARY · ADULT · LIBRARY

Look in the mirror. Then you can see your hair.

4

"Why can I see myself when I look in a mirror?"

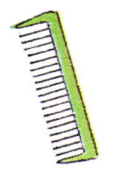

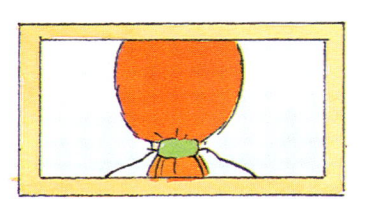

A mirror is made from glass that has a special shiny coating on the back. That's why mirrors reflect things.

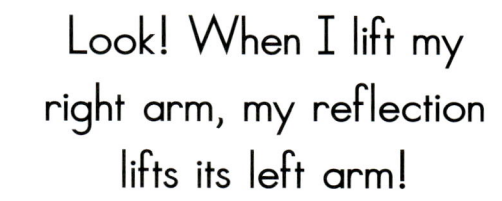

Look! When I lift my right arm, my reflection lifts its left arm!

Mirrors always reverse reflections. Right becomes left, and left becomes right.

This writing is backwards.

Mirror Magic

If you hold it up to a mirror, you will be able to read it.

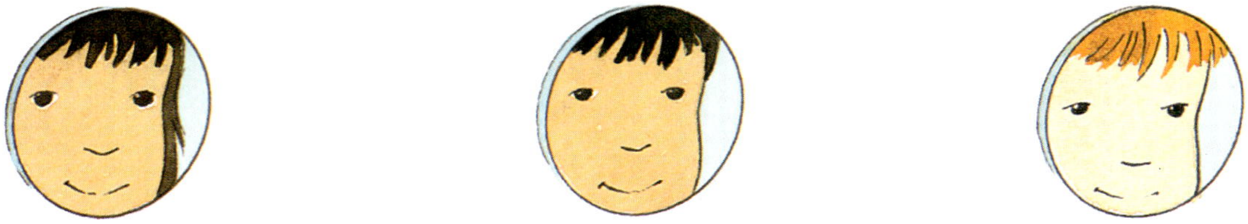

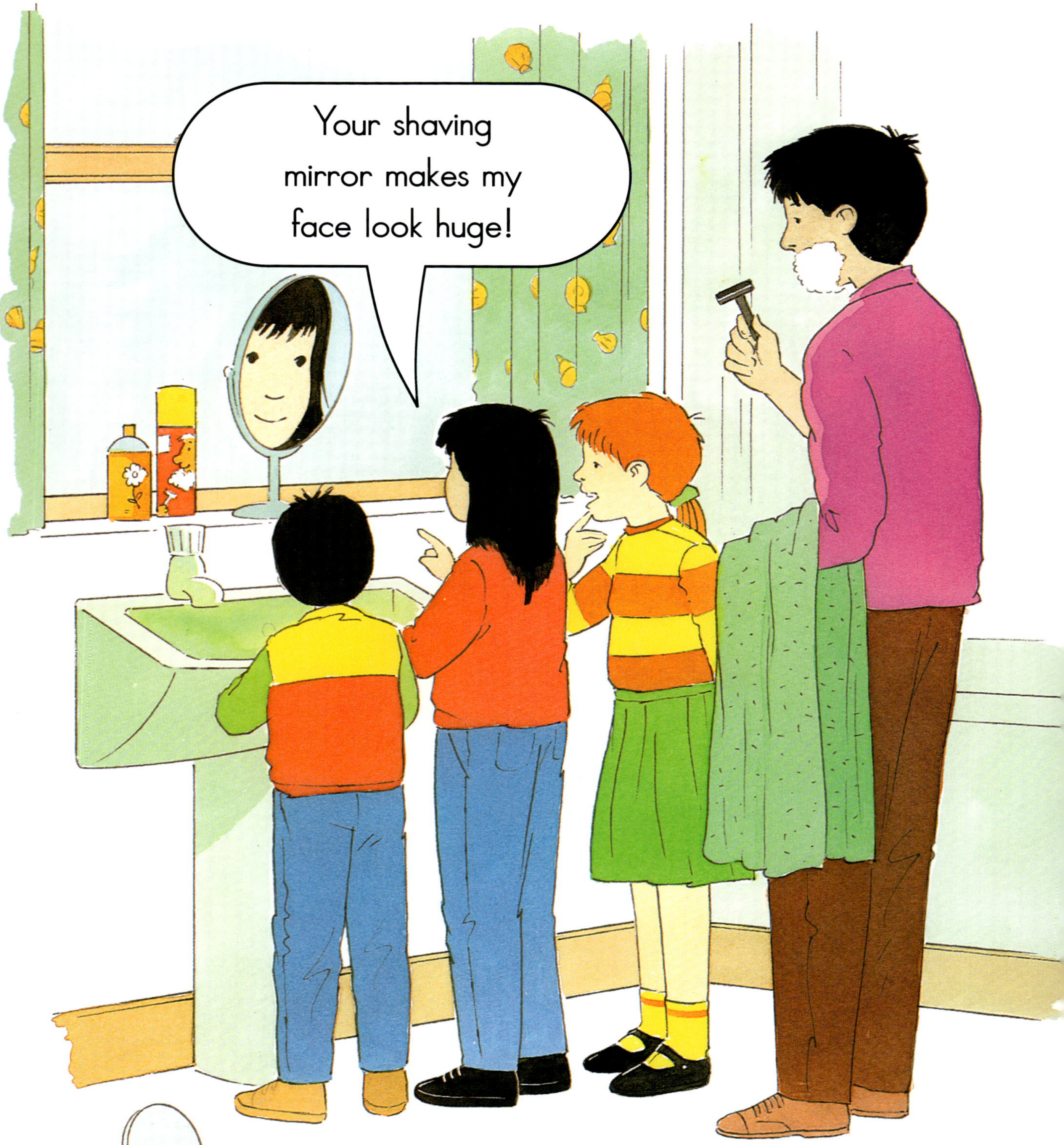
Your shaving mirror makes my face look huge!

It curves inward a little, which makes the things it reflects look larger than they really are. It's called a concave mirror.

"Can mirrors make things look smaller, too?"

Yes, mirrors that curve outward do that. They are called convex mirrors.

I saw one of those at a store. The clerk used it to watch customers.

11

A spoon can be used as a mirror, too. Look at yourself on the inside of the spoon.

I'm upside-down!

Now look at yourself on the back of the spoon. Spoons reflect light in a way that makes you look funny.

I'm a funny shape!

I've found another amazing thing that uses mirrors.
It's my kaleidoscope!

Inside a kaleidoscope, there are tiny mirrors. The patterns you see are made by bits of colored glass that have been reflected many times.

Let's go for a ride.
Dad, do you use that mirror on the outside of the car?

That's how he can see if cars come up behind us!

The mirrors on the outside of a car reflect other cars that are coming up on either side. These mirrors help people drive safely in traffic.

17

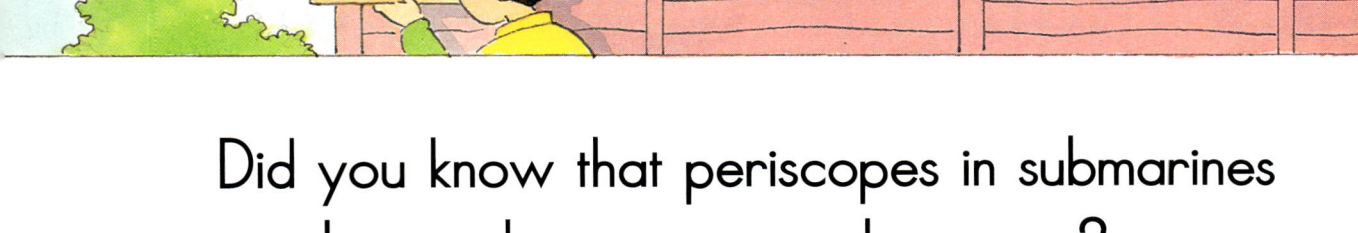

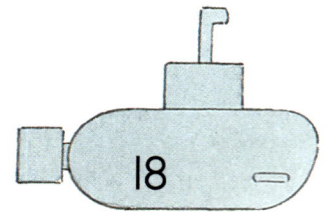

Did you know that periscopes in submarines can be used to see around corners?

"Do they have mirrors in them?"

Yes, they have two mirrors inside. Even if the submarine is underwater, the captain can still see ships floating on the surface.

Dad, why do you keep looking in the rearview mirror?

20

People use rearview mirrors to see the cars behind them. It could be dangerous if drivers kept turning around to look.

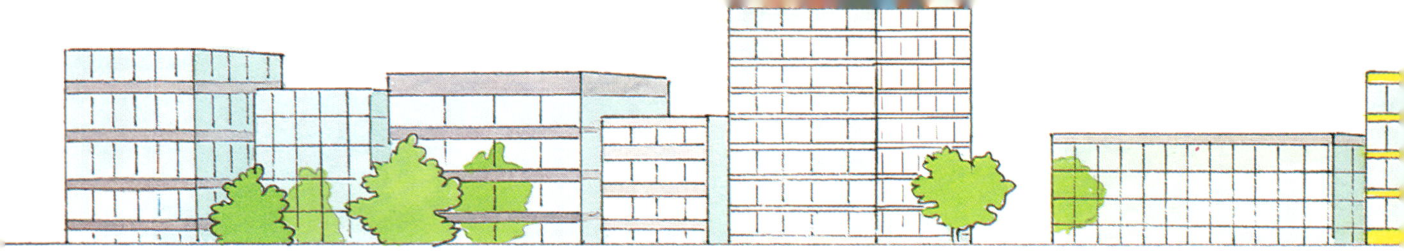

Wow! Look at those amazing buildings!
They look like they're made out of mirrors!

The windows are made of glass that acts like a giant mirror. They reflect the sky and the clouds.

Now we're at the carnival. This is the House of Mirrors.

I look short and round!

24

I look tall and thin!

People look strange here because all the mirrors are curved. Only flat mirrors give true reflections.

25

I can see my reflection in the pond!
Why does the water look blue?

The water looks blue because it reflects the sky. That's why the ocean looks blue on a clear day. When the sky is cloudy, the ocean looks gray.

Let me see what I look like.

You look funny!

Mirrors are very useful, but they can be fun, too.

What would we do without mirrors?

29

Where would you find these mirrors? The answers are on the next page, but don't look until you have tried naming the places.

1.

2.

3.

4.

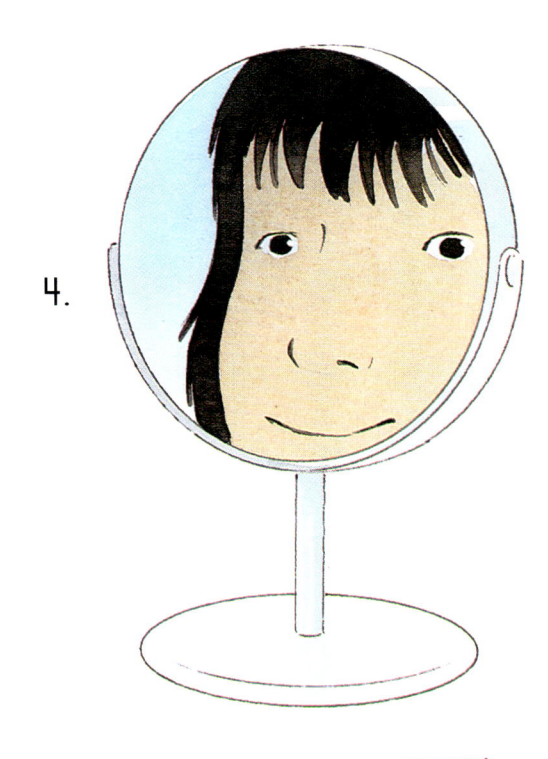

5.

Index

Kaleidoscopes **14-15**

Mirrors
 concave **8-9, 31**
 convex **10-11, 30**
 House of Mirrors **24-25, 30**
 outside **16-17**
 rearview **20-21, 30**

Periscopes **18-19**

Reflections
 changed **13, 24-25, 30**
 larger **8-9**
 reversed **6-7**
 smaller **10-11**
 true **4-5, 22-23, 28-29, 31**
 upside-down **12**

Water **26-27**

31

Answers: 1. In a House of Mirrors 2. In the car 3. In a store
4. In the bathroom 5. In a bedroom

32